Joe and Sparky, Superstars!

Joe and Sparky, Superstars!

Jamie Michalak

illustrated by Frank Remkiewicz

CANDLEWICK PRESS

To Julie.
And for Patrick and Finn—what a pair!
J. M.

For Alex
F. R.

Text copyright © 2011 by Jamie Michalak
Illustrations copyright © 2011 by Frank Remkiewicz

First paperback edition in this format 2013

The Library of Congress has cataloged the hardcover edition as follows:

Michalak, Jamie.
Joe and Sparky, superstars! / Jamie Michalak ; illustrated by Frank Remkiewicz.—1st ed.
p.   cm.
Summary: When Joe the giraffe and his friend Sparky, a turtle, see a television talent show,
Joe tries to find Sparky's talent so that they can compete.
ISBN 978-0-7636-4578-6 (hardcover)
[1. Ability—Fiction. 2. Friendship—Fiction. 3. Giraffe—Fiction. 4. Turtles—Fiction.]
I. Remkiewicz, Frank, ill. II. Title.
PZ7.M5815Jo 2011
[E]—dc22   2009006425

ISBN 978-0-7636-6642-2 (paperback)

13 14 15 16 17 18 SCP 10 9 8 7 6 5 4 3 2 1

Printed in Humen, Dongguan, China

This book was typeset in Adobe Caslon.
The illustrations were done in watercolor and colored pencil.

Candlewick Press
99 Dover Street
Somerville, Massachusetts 02144

visit us at www.candlewick.com

Contents

Chapter One
New Friends

In Safari Land, the famous cageless zoo, a turtle hid in his shell.

Not far away, a giraffe stretched his neck to see the world.

"Hop to it, Sparky!" said Joe Giraffe. "I see something fun. I will show you."

"I do not want something fun," Sparky said. "I want my warm rock."

"You are always on your warm rock," said Joe. "Come with me. We will have a super day!"

Joe lowered his head so Sparky could climb on top.

"OK," said Sparky. "But do *not* run!"

"Do not worry, my small, green, friend," said Joe.

Sparky climbed on. Joe ran.

"SLOW DOWN! SAFETY FIRST!"
Sparky yelled.

But Joe did not like slow. He ran as fast
as he could.

At the end of the road was a building. Joe and Sparky looked in a window.

"We are here!" said Joe. "See? This is something fun."

"It is a box," said Sparky. "Who are those small people in it?"

"They must live in the box," said Joe.

The small people danced.

OFFI

"They look happy to see us," Joe said. "Hello, small friends!"

"What are they saying?" asked Sparky. "Probably that we are their biggest friends ever."

The small people danced away. *Poof!*

Another small person popped into the box. **"WELCOME TO TV'S BEST TALENT SHOW, *WHAT A PAIR!* WATCH TALENTED TWOS TRY TO BE STARS!"** the small person shouted. **"I AM YOUR HOST, GRANT WISH!"**

Sparky jumped. "Why is he yelling at us?"

"MEET OUR FIRST SINGERS!" Grant Wish said.

Out came a small couple.

"OH, YEAH, BABY, BABY! OW!"

Sparky covered his ears. "*Ow* is right!"

Next came two small cheerleaders.

"Give me a *P*!" they shouted.

"I do not have a pea," said Joe. "Would you like a tasty leaf instead?"

They watched many talented pairs.

"HEY, YOU OUT THERE!" shouted Grant Wish. **"ARE YOU TIRED OF LIFE IN THE SLOW LANE?"**

"No," Sparky replied. "I am not."

"ARE YOU READY TO COME OUT OF YOUR SHELL?"

"Oh, my!" said Sparky. "That would be embarrassing."

"THEN JOIN US NEXT TIME AS WE LOOK FOR MORE TALENTED PAIRS!"

"Slam dunk!" said Joe. "Did you hear that, Sparky? They want us to join them!"

"Do you have a talent?" Sparky asked.

"Lots," said Joe. "I can run fast, wiggle my ears, and touch my nose with my tongue. Oh, and I can drive a car."

"I do not want a talent," said Sparky. "I want my warm rock."

"But I need you. We have to be a talented *pair*," Joe said. "Will you find your talent? Pretty please with ice cream and flies on top?"

Sparky hid in his shell to think. After a while, he poked his head out.

"Just for you," he said, "I will try. But a turtle is not a star. A turtle is a turtle."

"Do not worry," said Joe. "*I* will help you find your talent. You will be Sparky the Star. And I will be Joe the World's Best Talent-Finder."

CHAPTER TWO

The Dance Lesson

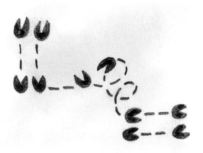

"Sparky, I think you were born to dance,"
said Joe. "I know *I* was. I will teach you
the Hokey Pokey. It is easy. First we form
a circle. Then you put your right legs in."

Joe put his right legs in.

"Then you put your right legs out,"
said Joe.

He put his right legs out.

"Joe, that is a *very* dangerous idea!" said
Sparky. "Turtles do not do wild things like
put their legs all over the place. Turtles
sit on warm rocks."

Joe frowned.

"But just for you," Sparky said, "I will try."
Very slowly, Sparky put his right legs in.

Joe watched Sparky dance. He ate some
leaves.

Very slowly, Sparky put his right legs out.
Joe watched. He ate LOTS of leaves.

"Phew. I need a break," said Sparky.
"How was that?"

"Good," said Joe. "Now you shake your
legs all about."

"Why?" Sparky asked.

"Because that is the Hokey Pokey. That
is what it is all about," Joe said.

Sparky grumbled. He raised his right legs again. He shook them all about.

"Look, I can dance!" Sparky said. "I do not believe it!"

Sparky shook his legs low. He shook his legs high. He shook his legs *too* high.

"HELP!" Sparky cried. He fell onto his shell.

"I do not think I was born to dance," said Sparky.

"No," Joe agreed.

"Maybe the Hokey Pokey is *not* what it is all about," said Sparky. "Not for turtles, anyway."

"That is the trouble with turtles," said Joe. "They do not Hokey Pokey. But some tell a good joke. Maybe you are funny. Like me. Let us find out."

Chapter Three
Sparky Tells a Joke

"Monkeys are funny," said Joe. "It is like I always say: if you want to be funny, copy a monkey."

Joe and Sparky visited the monkeys.

"Copy this monkey here," said Joe.

Sparky sighed. "Just for you, I will try."

The monkey made a silly face.

Sparky made a silly face.

The monkey jumped up and down.
Sparky tried to jump up and down.

The monkey threw a banana peel on the ground. He ran over the banana peel. *Whoops!* He slipped on the banana peel.

"Ha, ha!" Joe laughed. "That monkey is crazy. He is BANANAS!"

Sparky hid in his shell. "Being funny looks *very* dangerous. That monkey needs a safety helmet."

"You do not have to fall to be funny," Joe said in a hurry. "You can tell a joke. I will show you how. Knock, knock!"

Sparky looked around. "Knock on what?"

"You do not knock," said Joe. "You say, 'Who is there?' Then I say, 'Banana.'"

"Banana who?" asked Sparky.

"Knock, knock!"

"Who is there?" Sparky asked louder.

"Banana," said Joe.

"Joe! Do you have bananas in your ears?" Sparky said. "I already said 'Banana WHO?'"

"Knock, knock!" said Joe.

"WHO IN THE WORLD IS THERE?" Sparky shouted.

"Orange."

Sparky groaned. "Orange WHO?"

"Orange you glad I did not say banana?" Joe said.

The monkey made a mad face. He threw the banana peel at Joe's head.

"I do not think the monkeys like that joke," said Sparky. "Maybe they will like mine. Knock, knock!"

"Who is there?" asked Joe.

"Anita," said Sparky.

"Anita who?"

"Anita nap on a warm rock," said Sparky.

"You are right," said Joe. "Being funny is not your talent."

For the rest of the day, Joe searched for Sparky's talent.

Sparky tried racing.

He tried sliding.

And he tried balancing.
Sparky tried and tried
until the sun set.

"I am done!" said Sparky. "I cannot dance
or tell a joke. I cannot run, slide, or stand
on one foot. I cannot be Sparky the Star.
Just for you, Joe, I have tried. But we will
never be a talented pair."

"Of course we will," said Joe. "But this
might take a while. Let us go ask the small
people for more time."

Sparky did not move.

"Are you ready?" Joe asked Sparky.

"YES!" Sparky shouted. "I am ready to nap on my warm rock!"

"OK," said Joe. "Stars need their rest. But first things first."

Sparky grumbled. He climbed on top of Joe's head. Joe ran.

"SLOW DOWN! SAFETY FIRST!" yelled Sparky.

But as fast as he could, Joe ran to the end of the road.

CHAPTER FOUR
Sparky the Star

At the end of the road was the building. There was the box. But it was dark.

"Where did the small people go?" Sparky asked.

"Oh, no! They have packed up and left town," said Joe. "They must have been in some kind of small people circus."

"If there are no small people, then there is no show," said Sparky. "Phew! I do not need a talent anymore."

"This is a disaster," Joe said. "What will we do now?"

"We will go home," said Sparky.

"OK," Joe said sadly. "My pet worm, Wiggy, is waiting for me."

"Does Wiggy have a talent?" Sparky asked.

"Of course," said Joe. "He can make the letters *S* and *O* with his body."

"Wow! Could I meet this Wiggy?" said Sparky.

"Not today," said Joe. "He is a very busy worm."

It was dark when Joe dropped Sparky off at his warm rock.

"Look! Do you see my shadow?" said Joe.

"I will make a shadow puppet.

Can you guess what I am?"

Joe stood very straight.

"No," said Sparky.

"I am a flagpole," said Joe.

"I see," said Sparky. "Now can you guess what I am?"

"Hmm. That is a hard one. You are round. You do not move. Are you a warm rock?" Joe guessed.

"Yes!" said Sparky. "Now what am I?"

"That is hard, too. You are round.
You do not move. Are you a speed bump?"

"Right!" said Sparky. "What am I now?"

"Hmm. You are round. You do not move.
Are you a bump on a log?"

"Yes! Yes! Yes!" said Sparky. "You guessed
them all!"

"Slam dunk! Do you know what this
means?" said Joe. "You have a talent.
You make super shadow puppets!"

"It is a gift," said Sparky.

"Now we are both talented," said Joe.
"If only we had been able to show everyone."

Sparky looked behind him. His cheeks
turned red.

"But Joe," he said, "I think we just did!"

Joe turned around. He saw all their
animal friends. And the crowd went wild.

"Does this mean I am Sparky the Star?" Sparky asked.

"No," said Joe.

"No?" Sparky asked.

"No," said Joe. "You are Sparky the SUPERstar. Not everyone has a shadow like yours. Your shadow is one of a kind."

"You are one of kind, too, Joe. You are the World's Best Talent-Finder," said Sparky.

Joe smiled. "Good night, my small, green friend."

"Good night, Joe," said Sparky.

On a nice warm rock, Sparky hid in his shell. ZZZZZZZZ.

Not far away, Joe stretched his neck to see the world.